THE
ROCKING
CHAIR

THE ROCKING CHAIR

Edgar J. Hyde

CCP

ISBN 1 90201 221 6

Printed and bound in Scotland

Contents

Contents

Chapter One

Gerry turned over and looked towards his bedroom window. His bedroom curtains had been too small ever since his mother had decided to wash them in their own machine rather than take them to the shop down the road as she usually did. The bright yellow beam from the street lamp outside shone annoyingly through the gap that now existed between the two curtains, lighting up the far corner of Gerry's room. The very corner where his blow-up alien sat, staring across the room with its evil eyes. Gerry had loved it when he had seen it in the shops. He had thought it would be a great thing for scaring his little sister. She was scared of absolutely anything. But now it was giving him the creeps too, especially tonight with its weird yellow glow. It looked as though at any moment it would rise onto its legs, leap onto the bed, and blast Gerry away with one laser beam from its eyes.

Gerry tugged the quilt cover over the top of his head, rolled over, and tried to think of something else – the football team, the goal he scored last week, the new girl who had just moved in down the street (and who Gerry was trying to pretend to ignore but somehow had managed to walk past her house at least six times a day). It was useless. Gerry could feel the alien's stare through the quilt, digging into his back. He pulled the cover down, slowly, half expecting to see the alien right up next to him ready to pounce. He looked over to the corner. Nothing! The alien was gone! Gerry's heart started to race.

Gerry slowly raised his head, looking around, searching to find the evil bag of hot air, which now threatened his very life. Gerry pulled back the quilt and placed his feet on the floor, looking over at the bedroom curtains which were strangely swaying back and forth now.

"So there you are!" Gerry thought. He was starting to plan how he was going to get the better of his extra-terrestrial enemy. There was no way this piece of plastic was going to defeat him. Well, after all, he was the one who had spent half an hour blowing the creature up after his dad had ignored his pleas to do it for him.

Gerry stood up and reached over, pulling a dart from the dart board hanging over the top of his bed.

"This'll soon sort you out," Gerry thought. He looked over towards the window again. The curtains were still swaying slowly. Gerry was not very good at darts. The holes in the wall all around his dart board were proof of that. The distance between him and the curtains was double the normal distance he usually stood from a dart board. He had to get closer, but he wouldn't have much time. He was sure if he started to walk towards the window, the Alien would be on him in a flash and all would be lost. He decided he would take two quick steps, pull his arm back and launch the fatal arrow, all in one movement.

Gerry breathed in deeply, steadying himself for the challenge. He was sure he would only have one chance. If he missed, he would be lost, and his family would be next. He had to succeed, he had to get it right. But his legs seemed frozen to the floor.

"Come on, Gerry, pull yourself together. You have to do it," he thought, trying to summon up the courage.

He jumped forward, raising his arm, and fell, with a thump, in a heap on the floor, his legs tangled around some unknown obstruction. The dart flew high through the air and came to rest in the right eye of his school photograph, hanging on the wall.

Gerry lay flat on the floor. He turned his head and stared straight at the familiar piercing eyes of his blown up enemy. It was as lifeless as ever. The stupid thing had just slipped harmlessly to the floor. Gerry looked over at the curtains. He could now feel the gentle breeze entering the room through the slightly open window, causing the curtains to sway from side to side.

"What a prat," Gerry thought as he picked himself up. "You, my alien nemesis, are going in the bin in the morning," he muttered quietly as he picked the grey creature up and placed it back in the corner of the room. He looked at it one more time. The yellow tint from the street lamp threatening to recreate the same eerie atmosphere all over again.

Gerry moved over to the window and grabbed the two curtains, pulling them together, trying to block out the light. But no matter how hard he tried he couldn't close them completely. It was useless. They were simply too small. His mother had ruined them Gerry looked out at the offending street lamp and wondered if anyone would notice if he were to launch a brick at it in the morning, and put an end to his misery. Maybe that was not such a good idea, he thought, remembering how he had just been released from his latest "grounding" after he had managed to scratch his dad's new car when his bike had not stopped quite quickly enough at the end of a race with Stevie from next door.

Gerry looked out of the window. The street lamp lit up the whole street in a strange yellow/orange glow. His dad's car sat proudly in front of their house. Their's was one of the first cars in the street. He looked over to the other side of the road, where his sister had chalked on the pavement all the names of her friends. He could just make out "Sally James" the girl from No. 14. Gerry peered across. The house across the road had been empty ever since his family had moved into the street. It was in a terrible mess, practically falling apart. His mother had warned Gerry and his sister to stay away from it and there were all sorts of stories about it. Gerry stared hard. Something seemed to be moving. He pulled his curtains further back and pushed his face hard up against his window. There was definitely something moving. Gerry strained his eyes, the light from the street lamp barely reached the front of the house opposite.

Gradually Gerry began to make the image out. In the front porch of the old derelict house he could now clearly see an old man swinging back and forth, sitting in a rocking chair. Gerry looked at his bedside clock. It was 2.00 in the morning. What on earth was going on. He stared across, trying to recognise who this old man could be. As he looked across he suddenly saw the old man turn and look straight up at Gerry's window. A strange smile came to the old man's face, a smile that made Gerry's blood turn cold. The old man's stare was fixed, his narrow eyes piercing through the dimness.

Chapter One

For the second time that night Gerry's legs froze. He was unable to turn away from the figure facing him. Suddenly the old man raised his hand and started to wave as if beckoning Gerry to come to him. The old man's arm seemed to reach out, getting bigger and bigger, closer and closer, until the wrinkled hand seemed only inches away from the bedroom window. Gerry felt himself stagger back, falling . . . .falling . . . . .his lips barely managing to utter ". . . Dad . . . Dad . . . Dad!"

"Gerry . . . Gerry . . . wake up. It's alright son. It's only a bad dream. Don't worry."

Gerry opened his eyes to see his dad leaning over him, gripping his shoulders tightly, trying to console him.

"It's OK son. Calm down. You've only been dreaming," Mr Tooms said softly trying to calm his trembling son.

Gerry looked around. He was lying in his bed. His dad's large frame filled most of his view.

"What a noise you were making son . . . as if you had seen a ghost! Go back to sleep now, you'll be fine," Mr Tooms said, standing up and heading for the bedroom door.

"I told you that alien was a bad idea. That'll teach you," Mr Tooms joked as he closed the door behind him.

"Sleep well, son."

Gerry waited for a moment and then climbed out of bed, glancing briefly at his grey extra-terrestrial friend in the corner and walked to his bedroom window. He stared across the street at the old house opposite. The porch was empty. No rocking chair, no old man. He shook his head.

"What a night!" he thought. "You are definitely for the bin in the morning," he whispered as he slapped the unsuspecting alien across the head and climbed into bed.

"What a night!"

As Gerry closed his eyes, smiling to himself at his stupidity, he didn't notice the shadow swaying across his bedroom wall . . . The unmistakable shadow of a rocking chair!

Chapter Two

"Come on Gerry, it'll be good fun. No one will find out. Your mum's at the shops with your sister and your dad won't be home for ages."

Stevie Murphy was Gerry's best friend and lived at No. 22, right next door. He was always up to no good and always getting Gerry into trouble. It was Stevie who had let off the stink bomb in school last year, causing the whole second floor to be evacuated for an hour. It was Stevie who had thrown Gerry's sister's schoolbag onto a No. 65 bus as it was passing. It had taken them three days to get the schoolbag bag from the bus company. Gerry's mum had not been amused.

"Come on Gerry," Stevie shouted as they walked up the street towards their houses.

"We've never been in there before. Let's explore," Stevie continued, crossing the road and heading for No.19, the old derelict house that stood opposite their own.

"If we get caught we'll be in for it this time, Stevie," Gerry replied, trying to put his friend off.

The two boys stood outside the old rundown building, peering through the dirty, cracked windows, trying to summon up some courage. Gerry hadn't thought any more of the dream that he'd had the week before. His dad said he always talked in his sleep and was also prone to the occasional sleepwalking session. He'd grow out of it, he'd been told.

Gerry was more afraid of seeing his mother's face than that of any imaginary old man.

"Come on then – quickly. Let's go round the side, out of sight. We'll get in that way," Gerry said as he jumped over the rickety garden fence and disappeared round the corner.

Round the back of the house the garden was completely overgrown. The grass and weeds were almost as tall as the boys. To the side of the house was an old shed. An old iron drainpipe ran down from its roof.

"Stevie, up here," Gerry had already begun to clamber up the drainpipe on the shed wall and was almost on the shed roof. From there Gerry could reach a window on the side of the house, long without glass from numerous "missile" attacks from the boys on the street.

Within seconds the boys were inside.

"What a smell," Stevie whispered, pinching his nose.

"Yeah, reminds me of one of your famous stink bombs, Stevie," Gerry replied punching his friend on the arm. The two boys looked around at the empty shell of the house.

"You have a look up here. I'll go downstairs. Let me know if you find anything," Gerry instructed, heading for the stairs.

Gerry made his way down the stairs. The layout of the house seemed exactly like his own. He walked through the kitchen and into the adjoining dining room. Nothing. The place was completely empty. From there he went back into the hallway and on into the front sitting room. He walked over to the large bay window that looked out onto the porch. He wondered if there was any sign of his mother yet. She could be home at any time.

He reached over to the window and wiped some of the engrained dirt away with his jacket sleeve. His mother would kill him when she saw the colour of it. He pressed his face up against the window. But all he saw was the back of a head.

"Stevie, how did you get out there?" Gerry shouted tapping at the window with his fingers.

"Stevie, get back in here. My mum will be back any time. She'll see you," he added.

But there was no reply. Gerry looked harder. He rubbed away some more of the dirt from the window. He was beginning to get that "feeling" again. The one where his legs went wobbly and stuck to the spot.

Stevie didn't have grey hair. He wasn't wearing an old grey cardigan.

"Oh, oh!" Gerry thought.

Slowly the head turned around. Gerry started to recognise the old face from last week. The man began to smile at him.

Gerry staggered back. He ran out the room along the hall and bounded up the stairs, three at a time.

At the top he ran into Stevie coming out of one of the bedrooms. The two fell to the floor.

"What the . . . ?" Stevie moaned, lying flat on his back.

"Come on! Let's get out of here now! NOW, I said!" Gerry shouted, pulling his friend up. Within seconds they were out on the shed roof, scrambling down the drainpipe and sprinting across the road to the safety of Gerry's house. The two didn't stop until they had reached Gerry's room.

"What's got into you, you nutter?" Stevie gasped, his lungs struggling to recover. "There's no sign of your mother anywhere."

Gerry hesitated. He couldn't tell Stevie

what he had seen. He would just laugh at him.

"That place just gave me the creeps. It was boring anyway. Come on let's go down the park. Grab the football there." Gerry replied, trying to look as calm and composed as possible.

As the two boys made off down the street heading towards the park, Gerry's mind was racing. What was going on? Was he going crazy? He couldn't resist one last look. He glanced around. There he was. Waving. Rocking back and forth in his rocking chair. Smiling, that strange disconcerting smile.

"Come on, Stevie . . . last one down the park's a girlie!" Gerry shouted nervously as he made off at top speed, yards ahead of his unsuspecting friend.

That night, Gerry couldn't sleep. From his bed he kept on looking over towards his bedroom window but he couldn't summon up the courage to go over and have another look. Earlier, when they had been coming back from the park, he had planned to show Stevie what he had seen. But when they reached his house, and he had looked over to the derelict house, there was nothing there. The old man had disappeared again.

Gerry looked over once again to his window.

"This is crazy," he thought. "There must be some explanation for this."

He pulled his quilt back and slowly walked to the window. Without touching the curtains, he leaned over and looked out through the gap. There he was, looking up already, waving. Gerry stepped back, closed his eyes and shook his head. He moved forward and looked out again. The old man was still there but now he was sitting back, reading a paper, still rocking back and forth. For some reason, Gerry felt less threatened. Perhaps it was because he couldn't see the old man's face any more. It was hidden behind the large newspaper. Strangely, although the light in the porch opposite was very poor, Gerry could clearly see the front of the newspaper. The words seemed to have some strange luminous power that pierced through the dimness of the night.

It was as if the newspaper headlines were some sort of message to him. He started to whisper the words to himself.

"School Bus Crash. 5 injured."

The old man lowered the newspaper and looked up towards Gerry's window, the same twisted smile appearing on his face. He lifted his hand and started to wave. For some reason Gerry felt less threatened, less scared. As he looked across, the old man's image started to fade in front of his very eyes. Soon he was gone. The porch was empty. Gerry continued to look out for a few moments longer, but everything remained still.

Gerry turned around and climbed back into bed, the newspaper headlines repeating over and over again in his mind, until he could take no more and he drifted off to sleep.

"School Bus Crash. 5 injured . . . School Bus Crash. 5 injured . . . School Bush Crash. 5 injured . . . School Bus Crash. 5 injured . . ."

Chapter Three

Four days had passed since Gerry had last seen the old man in the porch opposite. He had hardly slept any night since, getting up six or seven times a night to look across to the old house. Each time he had seen nothing. He was beginning to feel it all had been a bad dream, or worse, some old tramp who had been using the place as a shelter for a while.

Gerry looked at the clock on his classroom wall 3.45 p.m. 15 more minutes to go, he thought. Football training tonight. Great. He had been selected again for the first team and was looking forward to the big Cup match on Saturday.

Eventually, the bell sounded and the

mad chaotic scramble for the door started.

"Don't run. Slowly!" Mrs Martin shouted in vain, shaking her head.

As Gerry ran down the corridor he spotted his sister, Susie. As he ran past her, he managed to pull her hair, slip her bag off her shoulder and trip her up, all in one slick movement. It was a well-practised manoeuvre.

"See you later, Sis. Remind Mum that I'll be home late after the footie," Gerry shouted, disappearing down the corridor, running and leaping up, heading an imaginary football.

Susie picked herself up and considered going after him, but he was gone.

"I'll tell Mum, alright. I'll tell her what an idiot you are," she muttered under her breath.

Gerry scored two goals, but managed to miss three penalties during football practice. So if the Cup game went to penalties he knew his services would not be asked for.

"But the keeper keeps moving," Gerry had pleaded to the coach

"What do you want him to do? Just stand there and let you slot it in the corner, son?" Mr Andrews had replied, smiling at him. "More practice Gerry, head over the ball," he had advised.

Gerry and Stevie walked up the street towards their houses recounting the evening's good moves, tackles and goals. Gerry looked over at the old derelict house. Nothing. Thank goodness. He smiled.

"See you tomorrow, Gerry. Remember . . . head down," Stevie goaded.

"See you, Stevie. Never mind, letting in seven goals isn't that bad!" Gerry replied pushing his friend away playfully.

Gerry opened his front gate and walked through. He looked up at his house. Strangely, it was in complete darkness. Where was everyone? He looked at his watch. 6.30 pm. Everyone should be here. His dad usually came home by 6.00 pm. Susie's music class is on Tuesdays. So everyone should have been in.

"Hello . . . anybody in?" He shouted, vainly.

But there was no reply. The house was empty.

"Aaah . . . what a pain!" Gerry muttered. He knew the routine now. His parents still wouldn't give him a key. He would have to sit out on the porch steps until someone came home.

"But where are they?" he thought. He was starving. His mum knew he was always starving after football training.

"What a pain!" He shouted, sitting

down on the top step and pulling out one of his football magazines from his bag.

Gerry didn't have to wait too long. About five minutes later he heard the familiar sound of his dad's car coming up the street. He stood up determined to look in as bad a mood as possible. He put on his best grumpy face.

However as soon as he saw his mum climb out of the car, his expression changed. He could tell something was wrong.

His mum was carrying Susie, wrapped in a blanket. Both of them had obviously been crying. Mr Tooms, Gerry's dad looked serious. He opened the gate and they all came through. Mr Tooms noticed his son standing on the porch steps and could see the look of concern on his face.

"It's alright son. She's going to be fine.

She's just had a nasty shock. We all have," Mr Tooms said solemnly

"But what happened?" Gerry quizzed as they walked by him to the door.

"Of course, you wouldn't have heard . . . football training. It was terrible, Gerry, son. The school bus crashed into a truck on the way home from school earlier. It was a real bad one. Susie's fine but they have kept five from her class in hospital overnight. They were very lucky. It could have been a lot worse," Mr Tooms replied, opening the door.

The words hit Gerry immediately. He spun round and looked at the porch opposite. There he was, rocking back and forth, smiling. Gerry throat was dry.

"Dad . . . Dad," he started. But Mr Tooms had followed his wife and daughter inside. In a moment the old man was gone and the porch left empty.

Chapter Three

The words were clear in Gerry's mind "School Bus Crash. 5 injured." The image of the newspaper headline burnt brightly in his mind.

"A coincidence?" Gerry thought, trying to make some sense of the situation. His Mum and Dad were too concerned about Susie to listen to any harebrained stories from him. There was no point in telling them what he had seen, or what he believed he had seen. They would think he was crazy. He went inside and decided to think more about it later. His stomach was still crying out for food and was, for the moment, winning the battle over his mind.

Gerry stood at his bedroom window and looked across the street. This was the third time he had woken up. He couldn't get the newspaper headlines out of his head. He looked out again. There he was, at last.

The chair was slowly swaying back and forth. The old man looked up and smiled. He then leaned back and lifted his newspaper up again. As before, the words on the front page seemed to penetrate the darkness and were as clear as though they were made of neon lights.

"Cup victory for local school. 5-4 on penalty shoot-out."

There was a photograph below the headline that Gerry could just make out. It was of a football team. Gerry could make out the familiar black and white stripped shirts. It was his football team!

The image of the old man began to fade. Before disappearing he gave Gerry one last smile.

"This is crazy!" Gerry uttered out loud. But his thoughts immediately moved to Saturday and the big cup match against the team from the next town. His school had never beaten them. It was always a big crunch match.

"No . . . it would be impossible!" he whispered to himself as he climbed back into bed. "Impossible . . ."

Saturday couldn't come fast enough The whole school was buzzing with excitement and the boys were allowed an extra free class to do some more football training for the big match. Gerry couldn't make up his mind whether he should tell Stevie or not. How could he say that he'd received a message that his school was going to beat a team they had never beaten for about 25 years. Ridiculous. How could he explain the message he had been given?

Eventually the big day came and as Gerry stood out in the middle of the park it seemed as though the whole school were there. The noise was tremendous. Gerry looked back at Stevie in goals.

"Three will do, Gerry boy. You can do it," Stevie shouted to his friend, his two hands cupped around his mouth

The game seemed to pass in a flash. Chance after chance and save after save. But after ninety minute nobody had scored. The referee blew for the start of extra time. Everyone seemed to be getting more and more nervous and it wasn't long before the referee blew for the end of the game. Penalties.

One by one the penalties went in until the score stood at 4-4. Nobody had missed. The big centre-forward of the opposition walked up. He placed the ball on the spot and took a few paces back. Stevie crouched down, his body swaying from side to side. The big No. 9 ran forward and smacked the ball to Stevie's left. The rest of the team watched from the centre circle. It was as if it was all in slow motion. Stevie's body and outstretched arm moved to his left. The ball was heading right in the bottom corner. It looked a certain goal, until Stevie's fingertips blocked its path sending it round the post. The place went crazy . . . cheering and shouting, and then quickly there was silence. There was one more penalty to be taken. Everyone seemed to be holding their breath.

Mr Andrews walked up behind Gerry and tapped him on the shoulder.

"You're up, son. Give it your best."

"But-but," Gerry stammered

"Just keep your head down . . . on you go," Mr Andrews prompted, prodding Gerry forward.

Gerry picked up the ball and made his way up to the penalty area. The walk from the centre circle seemed to take forever. His legs felt like jelly. "Why me?" he thought.

He knew what the old man's newspaper had read, but he was hopeless at penalties.

He placed the ball, stepped back, breathed deeply, ran forward, closed his eyes and blasted it. A second later the noise was deafening. When he opened his eyes the goalkeeper was sprawled out on the ground and the ball was nestling in the back of the net. 5-4. They had done it!

As Gerry was lifted high on the shoulders of his team-mates, he thought of the old man on the porch. This was all very strange; very strange.

Chapter Four

Over the next few weeks Gerry had seen the old man four more times. Each time the old man had held up the newspaper and shown Gerry a different headline, and each time, within days of reading the headline, it had come true.

Firstly there was the fire at Beacon's farm, then the old lady in the next road had strangely fallen down the stairs, killing herself. Then there was the strange report of ghostly noises in the Church hall. The last incident was about the man who had been confronted by some "being" on the way home from work, late at night. It had frightened the life out of him. But no one believed him and everyone thought he had probably visited a pub on the way.

All of these had been headlines in the old man's paper a few days before they really happened and actually were reported in the local newspaper, written using the exact same words as in the old man's paper.

Gerry couldn't keep such information to himself any more. But no one would believe his story without proof. He decided that it was best to wait until he saw another headline from the old man. He would then tell the editor of the local newspaper about it and when it came true, everyone would understand the strange powers of the old man in the house across the road.

Gerry didn't have to wait too long for the next message. That very next night as he gazed out his bedroom window, he saw the image of the old man appearing. The old man looked up. He stared straight at Gerry. It was as if he could look right through him and read his mind. The old man wasn't smiling this time. He started to shake his head. Gerry wondered why the old man was acting differently.

The old man lifted the newspaper again and revealed his latest message to Gerry. Once again the words were clear. "Town clock struck by lightning – midnight Sunday night"

The message was obvious. The next day after school he went straight to the offices of the local newspaper. "The Weekly News." Eventually the editor agreed to see him. Gerry told the editor nothing about the old man but explained that he was convinced he had a way of telling the future. The editor listened to the boy and politely suggested that perhaps he should talk to his parents about his unique "gift". Gerry persisted and in the end the editor agreed to put a cameraman on duty on Sunday night to photograph the lightning strike, if it were to happen. The editor told Gerry to go home and come back and see him on Monday. They would know then if anything had happened.

On Sunday night, Gerry couldn't sleep. He quietly slipped on some clothes and crept out of his room, down the stairs, and out the front door. He had to see this for himself this time. He walked quickly to the town square. In the middle he could see the photographer setting up his equipment. It was a cold night and he could hear the photographer mutter away, obviously unhappy to be sent out on a cold night what he thought would be some wild goose chase. Gerry walked over to him.

"Hi," Gerry whispered.

"Good God! What the . . . ?" The photographer stammered, obviously startled by Gerry's approach.

"What are you doing here? What do you want?" The photographer quizzed.

"I'm here to see the lightning," Gerry answered smiling.

"How do you know about the . . . ?" the photographer hesitated and then continued, "Aahh . . . you're the lad who has got me out on this waste of time, come to see for yourself what an idiot you are. Look . . . not a cloud in the sky! Can't see any lightning coming from that!" The photographer snapped, nodding his head skywards.

Gerry looked at the sky. It was totally clear. For the first time he started to worry about his prediction. Surely the old man wouldn't let him down. He looked at the clock. Ten minutes to go.

The minutes passed slowly, and then Gerry watched as the hand clicked into position. 12 o'clock. Nothing. No thunder, no lightning, no hint of anything. Gerry and the photographer looked at each other and then at the sky. Nothing. The two waited on until finally, after about twenty minutes, the photographer spoke,

"Go home now, son. Put all these daft ideas out of your head, before you become a laughing stock."

The photographer packed up his stuff and headed off. Gerry turned away and headed home. He was confused. This was the first time that the old man's headlines had been wrong. Why? Why had it all gone wrong? No one would believe him now.

As Gerry turned into his street, he looked over to the old derelict house. The porch was empty. Why had the old man let him down this time? And then he remembered the old man shaking his head. Was he warning him that the headline this time was not true? But why give him the headline at all? Then it struck Gerry. This was the first time he had tried to tell anyone else. He had told no one about all the other headlines.

But if he couldn't tell anyone about the headlines, how was he going to get anyone to believe him? It was impossible.

Gerry crept back into his house and climbed into bed. What would he do now? He tossed and turned. Then he thought of an idea. It just might work. The next time the old man shows him a headline, he would say nothing to anyone. The time after that he would tell Stevie. If the first came true and the second didn't, he would know that he was trapped alone in this nightmare, unable to get anyone to believe him.

The very next night, the old man was there on the rocking chair, on the porch opposite. He held up the paper.

"Local train de-railed. Strange green fluid found on rails."

Gerry was immediately concerned. Loads of people could be injured. But what could he do? If he told anyone they would never believe him, and because he told them it probably wouldn't happen. What a position he was in!

Gerry spent the next few days nervously watching the news. Then it happened. The TV programme he and his sister were watching was interrupted with a News Flash

The announcer spoke solemnly

"We interrupt this programme to bring you news of a serious train crash, just outside Carswell village. Several people have been seriously injured. The cause of the accident is unknown at this time. More news later."

The next morning Gerry picked up the local paper as soon as it was delivered.

"Local train derailed. Strange green fluid found on rails." There it was. Exactly as it had been written on the old man's newspaper. Well, his theory seemed right so far.

A few days later, the old man appeared again. This time the headline read

"Teacher badly burned in mysterious fire." Below the headline was a picture of Mr Andrews the school PE teacher.

The next day as soon as Gerry saw Stevie, he told him he believed he could tell the future. Once again he mentioned nothing about the old man. He knew he ran the risk of looking like a right fool to his best friend. But he had no choice. If he were right, nothing would happen to Mr

Andrews because Gerry had told Stevie. Gerry would look daft but at least Mr Andrews would be safe and Gerry's theory would be proved true.

Gerry described to Stevie how he believed Mr Andrews was going to be badly hurt in a fire and told him he was convinced it would happen in the next few days. Stevie of course thought Gerry was talking nonsense and just laughed at Gerry's story. But Gerry was his best friend and he didn't want to hurt his feelings too much, so he said nothing to anyone else.

The days passed and Mr Andrews turned up for work day after day as normal, safe and sound and without injury. After a week Gerry was convinced. The old man's headlines only come true if they are kept a secret. If anyone else is told they simply don't happen. Stevie said nothing more to his best friend. If he wanted to act daft it was up to him.

Gerry returned to his room that day. When it was dark. He went to the window. The old man sat on the porch, rocking away. This time there was no newspaper. The old man just looked up and smiled. Then he faded away.

"What next?" Gerry wondered to himself. He wouldn't have long to wait to find out.

Chapter Five

"Susie, turn that down, will you? What a noise!" Gerry shouted, "I'm trying to do my homework!"

"I will not! Do your homework downstairs," Susie shouted back petulantly.

"Mum, will you tell her?" Gerry shouted, moving to the top of the stairs.

"Will you two stop shouting? For goodness sake give us some peace and quiet!" Mrs Tooms screamed back, almost breaking the sound barrier.

Gerry and Susie recognised her tone and ran back to their rooms, closing their doors behind them.

Mrs Tooms headed back to the sitting room, but before she was able to sit down and pick up her paper again the front doorbell rang.

"Oh, for crying out loud, what now? Can I not get a moment's peace?" she muttered, heading for the front door.

"Yes, can I help you?" Mrs Tooms asked, putting on her best welcoming smile.

"Mrs Tooms?" the visitor asked in return.

"Yes, I am Mrs Tooms. What can I do for you?" she replied

The visitor pulled an ID badge out of his pocket and held it up in front of him.

"Zebediah Moot from the The Weekly News. I'd like to talk to your son, if that's possible?"

Mrs Tooms looked at the ID badge and then back at the man standing on her doorstep. She smiled, remembering the photographs of Gerry in the paper a couple of weeks before. Her son had become quite a local hero since he scored that penalty.

"I'll get him for you. Please wait a moment," Mrs Tooms suggested, turning away, beginning to feel a bit of a celebrity herself.

She ran up the stairs and opened Gerry's door.

"Gerry, Gerry, come downstairs, the local newspaper wants to talk to you. This is so exciting," Mrs Tooms said beginning to get herself in a bit of a tiz.

Gerry looked at his mother, puzzled. "What do they want?" he asked

"I don't know, do I? Probably a follow up about the football match. Come on, hurry yourself, the man is waiting," Mrs Tooms said, her arms ushering Gerry out of his room.

Gerry followed his mother down the stairs and into the sitting room. Gerry looked over to the visitor who was standing facing out of the window. Slowly the man turned around.

"Hello, Gerry," he said smiling.

Gerry froze, his chin almost dropping to the floor. The same grey hair, grey cardigan. It was the old man from across the road.

"What's wrong with you, Gerry? Where are your manners?" Mrs Tooms piped up.

Gerry couldn't speak

"Don't worry Mrs Tooms. The lad hasn't quite got used to being in the limelight yet. He's only nervous. Not every day you get your name in the papers. Is it son?" Mr Moot interrupted.

Gerry shook his head. He couldn't believe the image he had seen so many times at night was now standing in his front room.

Chapter Five

"Mrs Tooms, do you mind if I take young Gerry down to the office? I'd like to have a good chat with him, background stuff, you know?" Mr Moot asked, putting his arm around the now shaking boy.

"Of course not, Mr Moot. Gerry, now, you tell Mr Moot all he needs to know. And remember your manners!" Mrs Tooms replied flushed with the excitement of it all.

Gerry thought that perhaps he should make a dash for it. He had no idea what this Mr Moot was up to. But even if he had wanted to run, Moot's arm was tightly round his shoulders.

Gerry considered the situation. Despite the weird events of the last couple of weeks the old man hadn't caused him any harm so far. If he didn't go with him, perhaps he would never find out what it was all about.

"Don't worry son, nobody's going to hurt you," Moot said, looking straight into Gerry's eyes. The same smile that Gerry was used to seeing from his bedroom window. It didn't exactly make him feel reassured.

Gerry opened his mouth and nervously stammered. "OK . . . let's. . . let's g-g-go."

With his arm still tightly round the boy's shoulder, Moot steered Gerry out the front door and down the garden path. Gerry looked nervously back at his mother who stood smiling at the front door, unaware of her son's frame of mind or predicament.

When the two of them had disappeared round the corner and out of sight of the house. Gerry spun round shaking off Moot's arm.

"Right then. What's your game?" Gerry demanded. He tried to hide the fear that was consuming his body.

But the old man just smiled.

"This isn't funny . . . isn't funny at all," Gerry continued. "What do you want?"

The old man looked at Gerry. "I want you of course, Gerry." With that he started to walk on leaving Gerry standing looking shattered and bemused.

Gerry looked at the old man as he headed off down the road.

"Me?" He thought. "He wants me?" Gerry felt even more concerned, but couldn't let the old man get away. He started to run and soon caught up with him.

"What do you mean, you want me? What are you up to?" Gerry demanded, standing in front of the old man blocking his path.

"Later, son, be patient. Follow me," Moot replied, stepping around the boy and continuing along the street.

Gerry followed after him keeping a couple of paces behind. No more was said.

After about ten minutes of walking, Moot turned into a side street and up to a large door. Gerry looked at the sign on the door.

"The Weekly News."

It was the offices of the local paper. Moot took out a key, unlocked the door and went in. Gerry followed.

As they walked up the main stairs and through the rows of desks Gerry realised the place was empty, completely empty. There wasn't a soul in the place.

Gerry looked at his watch 7.10 pm.

"Of course, its after hours. Everyone will have gone home," he thought to himself.

Finally Moot opened the door to a large corner office and walked in. Again, Gerry followed. Moot walked round a large oak desk and threw himself down on a huge, high-backed leather chair.

Gerry looked at the desk. In the middle stood a triangular wooden plaque with the words "Editor" inscribed on it.

"What are we doing here?" Gerry asked, finally summoning up the courage to speak again.

"This is my office, Gerry, make yourself at home. Grab a chair," Moot replied smiling smugly again and lighting up a cigar.

"But this . . . this is . . ." Gerry stammered.

"This IS my office," Moot leaned forward, his smile disappearing. "Now listen, Gerry, what I am about to tell you will appear unbelievable to you, but it is all true. Every last word. You must believe me," he added.

Gerry looked at the old man. Suddenly

his face seemed serious. His expression less threatening, less sure. His tone more pleading.

Moot continued, "I was the editor here once, and a great editor too, until HE got me," Moot seemed to nod his head upwards in no particular direction, as if to indicate some absent enemy.

"I was on to him, I almost had him. But he got to me first. I don't know how he did it, but he did."

"What are you talking about?" Gerry interrupted. The old man's words made no sense to him at all.

"The Ghost of Carswell Hall!" Moot exclaimed, thumping his fist on the desk and causing Gerry almost to jump out of his chair.

"The what?" Gerry asked.

"The Ghost of Carswell Hall, my boy. I was onto him. I had to stop him. He was terrorising the whole place. The town was becoming impossible to live in. Take a look at these."

Moot opened a drawer in the desk, pulled out some pieces of paper and threw them over to Gerry. Gerry looked at them. They were old newspaper clippings from years previous. Gerry read out the headlines one by one.

"Family die in unexplained fire", "Strange illness kills child", "Farmer's cows drowned in river", "Church tower falls, many injured."

"They were all down to him. He was the culprit, and there were many more. That was just some of them."

Moot turned away, his head in his hands. Gerry began to see tears running down the old man's cheeks.

Moot spun round. "They all thought I was crazy . . . wouldn't believe me. But he had to be stopped, people were leaving the town. They thought it was a curse or something. But I saw him. I spoke to him. It was him or me. I thought I had got rid of him, but he got me! He killed me as I sat on my own rocking chair, in my own house, and now he is back!"

Gerry could see that the old man was serious. He swallowed hard,

"But . . . but . . . what has this all to do with me?" He asked, somehow afraid to hear the answer.

"The town is in danger again, Gerry. No one is safe. I was the ghostbuster then Gerry. I failed. I am too weak now," Moot said slowly, his voice dropping to a whisper.

"You, Gerry, you must be the ghostbuster now," he continued solemnly, "The safety of the town is in your hands now."

Chapter Six

Moot's words were still ringing in his ears as Gerry walked slowly back home. No sooner had he said them than he seemed to vanish, leaving Gerry alone in the editor's office. Moot's story seemed ridiculous and yet he had to believe it. This ghostly old man was definitely real. Gerry knew he wasn't imagining him.

Certainly some of the recent events in the town were very strange. People were beginning to talk again about a curse. He had even overheard his mother and father talking about it a few days ago. He had heard his father laughing it off as some old wives' tale. But now there was another explanation, a much more sinister explanation. The whole situation was incredible and Gerry found himself right in the middle of it. He thought back to the night his sister was almost killed in the bus crash.

The lorry driver involved had said his steering wheel had just seemed to take control of itself and veer off, ploughing the heavy truck straight into the school bus. Nobody could explain it.

The more Gerry thought about it, the more he realised that people were in danger. His own family were in danger. His fear started to turn into anger. He thought of his crying sister again and the shocked face of his mother as she carried her home. He heard Zeb Moot's words again in his ears,

"You must be the ghostbuster now."

Gerry started to walk more quickly, more purposefully. He started to feel strong and brave. He started to feel special, somehow chosen. He walked on, totally unaware of the strange dark shadow that was following him, hugging the sides of the buildings where the street lights failed to reach. Darkness had quickly fallen, and the moon was struggling to break out from behind the dark clouds that covered the sky.

Gerry looked around. He had no idea how long he had been away from home. He seemed to have been in the newspaper offices for only a few minutes but somehow hours seemed to have passed. He suddenly felt vulnerable again. He walked on. This time he sensed something. He started to walk quicker. He could feel it. There was a presence. He felt uncomfortable. He stopped and looked around. Nothing. He started to walk more quickly. The street lamps once again cast an eerie glow across his path. He started to run.

He seemed to be running as fast as he could, but somehow he was getting nowhere. He stopped and turned around. He looked over to the other side of the road. He could see it now, the dark shadow. It seemed to hover, and then glide along, effortlessly. Gerry couldn't move. His muscles refused to respond. Fear had taken over his body again The shadow started to move towards him. It seemed to begin to take a form. A black hood, a long cloak. It began to move more quickly now sliding silently across the road . . . faster . . . faster, coming straight towards him. Gerry was frozen with fear. The strange vision was only a few yards from him now. Suddenly it stopped, hovering right in front of him. Gerry tried to speak, but his throat and mouth were bone dry.

Slowly the dark figure raised one arm and began to pull back its hood. Gerry's eyes bulged in terror. In front of him was a face, half skeleton and half rotten flesh, skin dangling from infested bones. The smell was overpowering. Its mouth opened and out crawled thousands of black ants. They poured out continuously. The creature began to laugh, louder and louder, louder and louder until the noise filled Gerry's head and started it spinning. Gerry's vision went out of focus and his legs began to wobble. He lost consciousness and fell to the ground.

Gerry had no idea how long he had been out. As he picked himself up, he looked around. The street was quiet. There was no sign of anyone. He rubbed the back of his head. He could feel the lump beginning to grow where his head must have thumped the ground. His heart was still racing. The street was brighter now. Gerry looked up. The clouds had disappeared and the moon was brightening up the sky. Gerry started for home, shaken and disturbed by the evening's events. His earlier determination to deal with these eerie goings on was dented by the strange visitation he had just experienced.

As he turned into his street, he looked over to the old derelict house. He could see the rocking chair swaying. He strained his eyes to make out the figure of the old man. But he couldn't see his usual grey hair. Everything seemed so black. Gerry started to walk over. He needed to get more answers out of Moot. But as he approached the house he froze. The image in the rocking chair began to look familiar. The same hooded spectre he had seen only a few moments earlier was sitting in the chair. It stood up and turned towards Gerry. The hood fell back slowly. It was Moot.

"If you are going to take my place, Gerry, you are going to have to be stronger and braver," the old man declared, shaking his head.

"You . . . you!" Gerry shrieked, his hand forming a fist.

"You must be stronger son to have any chance of winning. Go home. Get stronger. Prepare yourself. I will test you more. When you are ready we will fight him," Moot declared, sitting back down in the chair and rocking it back and forth.

Gerry started to walk away, slowly, backwards at first, afraid to look away from the old man. Finally He turned round and looked at his own house. The lights of the rooms looked so welcoming. He needed to feel safe now. He looked back at the old house. Moot was gone. The porch was empty. Gerry ran across the road and into the safety of his home.

Chapter Seven

"Well, Gerry, what's the answer? We're all waiting," Mrs Martin quizzed impatiently.

"Gerry, are you listening?" She demanded becoming increasingly irritated.

Gerry was in another world. He hadn't been able to concentrate all morning. Stevie had not managed to get a word out of him on the way to school, and now his mind was full of the strange goings on of the previous day.

"Gerry!" Mrs Martin had finally lost her patience.

Gerry looked up, the spell that held him seemingly broken.

"Sorry, Miss. What did you say?" Gerry asked, realising he was in bother.

"Gerry, I don't know what's wrong with you this morning. Your school project . . . remember? Finland? What's the capital?"

Gerry tried to concentrate, tried to put everything else from his mind.

"Helsinki, Mrs Martin," he replied, sitting up and trying to look his best attentive self.

"Well finally. Thank you Gerry," Mrs Martin commented, obviously unimpressed by Gerry's behaviour.

"Right, everyone, get your workbooks out, time for some algebra," Mrs Martin announced, turning to the blackboard and starting to wipe it clean.

There was a loud groan from the assembled class. Algebra was not popular. Mrs Martin loved putting them all to the test with some horrible equations that only one or two of them ever seemed to get right.

Gerry smiled. He was one of the chosen few. He loved algebra. Time to concentrate. He had to make sure he got more right than Stevie did.

He lifted the lid of his old worn out desk, and then let out an almighty scream. Hundreds of dirty grey rats clambered out of his desk, and started to climb onto him, up his arms, down his legs, on his face and over his head. Gerry flayed his arms about, trying to get the creatures off him. But as quickly as he pulled them off, more poured out of his desk. They were all over him. He couldn't get them off. He fell to the ground rolling about, crying for help at the top of his voice. They seemed to be everywhere. They were running up his trousers, down his jumper. He could feel them tearing at his skin, nibbling away with their tiny sharp teeth. The noise of them squealing and squeaking deafening him.

In a moment they were gone, as quickly as they had appeared. The ringing in Gerry's ears disappeared. Gerry looked around. The class were looking at him in stunned silence. He looked up. Mrs Martin was standing over him, hands on her hips, her face distorted in a deep frown.

"What on earth is going on Gerry? Is this some kind of joke?" Mrs Martin exclaimed, her patience with Gerry completely gone. She looked down on the ridiculous position the boy was in. His head and shoulders were under the desk, his chair had been kicked several yards away and his feet and legs were sprawled behind him.

"Pick yourself up, boy. Wait outside the classroom. I'll have a word with you in a moment," she snapped, pointing towards the door.

Gerry climbed to his feet and dusted

himself down. He could sense his classmates' sniggers and smirks. He could feel his face redden with embarrassment. They had seen nothing. It was all in his mind, or some trick played by Moot again. He wanted to get out of the room as quickly as possible. He strode towards the door, his legs still shaking from the attack. As he opened the classroom door he looked back. They were coming after him again, hundreds of rats were scurrying across the floor racing towards him. He slammed the door shut, pressing his back hard against it. Gerry closed his eyes and tried to calm himself down. He could hardly catch his breath.

The corridor was silent, peaceful. He looked to his left . . . nothing. He turned to his right . . . just in time to see the old man turn the corner.

"Moot!" Gerry snarled under his breath.

It had all been another test, another vision to scare him. Moot was trying to prepare him, to strengthen him. Gerry felt anything but strong, he was a bag of nerves. He started to pace up and down the corridor, trying to gather his thoughts. Moot was obviously trying to scare him. This had to be his way of strengthening him. If he was going to take on this ghost he would have to be able to handle fear better. He had to be able to cope with anything he might see. The way Moot had described the ghost, it was clear that he was very dangerous. If he couldn't control himself when confronted by the ghost, there was no way he would be able to win.

Gerry began to feel better. He had to control his emotions more. Moot would try to scare him again. The next time he would be prepared. He would be stronger.

He was just starting to feel like his normal self, when he heard the classroom door open and saw Mrs Martin walk out.

After school, Gerry sat on the steps outside the main entrance. He was thinking about the lecture he had just been given by the Deputy Head.

"You need to concentrate, lad . . . you need to get this nonsense out of your head . . . too much fooling around . . . important time of your life."

His thoughts were broken by the welcoming screeches of his friend Stevie, who was standing outside the school gates with a football under his arm.

"Come on move yourself, Gerry boy. We are late. Practice starts in five minutes," Stevie shouted, starting to play keepie-up with his head.

Gerry picked himself up. It would be

good to kick the ball around for a while. It would take his mind off things. He looked around, though, as he headed over to the school playing area to join his friend. He had to remain vigilant. He didn't want Moot to catch him out again.

"Right then, let's go. Give me the ball then?" Gerry demanded holding out his hand.

Stevie, threw the ball over. Gerry watched it in mid air as it flew towards him. He stretched to catch it before it fell. Just as it reached his hand the ball changed shape. Its roundness becoming longer and thinner. Gerry looked at his hand. He was now holding in his palm a black, hissing snake, its face distorted, its mouth open, displaying large, deadly fangs.

Gerry was about to jump away, launching the snake far from him. But he hesitated. Instead he gripped the snake tight and pulled it closer to him. He raised its face to his. He looked it in the eye and stared at it.

"Not this time," he whispered, almost a hiss to match the snake's. He threw the snake calmly to the ground. Before it reached the ground, it's shape starting to change again.

Gerry watched the ball bounce across the street. He turned to his friend. Stevie was nowhere to be seen. In front of him stood the old man, smiling as ever. Gerry was aware that there was no one else around.

"Well done son, you're learning. Come over to the porch tonight, after dark. We'll talk then," Moot said quietly.

"Gerry, Gerry, get a move on!" Gerry turned round and saw Stevie running up the street. He turned to the old man.

"Go on, don't worry . . . I'm off duty

now . . . no surprises," he prompted, smiling.

"Remember tonight. I'll be waiting."

Stevie came up to his friend, gasping for breath. "What's getting into you these days. Everyone is down at the park. Come on!"

Gerry turned and followed his friend. He felt good. He was getting stronger. He had managed to control himself. He was beginning to actually relish the challenge ahead.

Chapter Eight

Gerry stared out his window for what seemed like an eternity. His parents had gone to bed ages ago. His eyes were beginning to hurt, peering through the dull light towards the house across the road. Finally he could see the image. But now, he was taking it in his stride. He had really toughened up over the last few days.

"Sit down here, son, at my feet. Keep out of sight."

Moot beckoned to Gerry, pointing to the floor next to his chair. Gerry sat down. The old man leaned forward. He spoke slowly and deliberately.

"Gerry, I need you to help me. We have to destroy him once and for all. As I am from the spirit world now, I cannot do it on my own. I need your help. He can see my every move. He cannot see yours."

It was the first time, the old man had confirmed he was a ghost. Now, he was taking it in his stride. After all that had happened to him over the last few days, nothing was likely to surprise him now. He had really toughened up over the last few days.

"But, who is he? What is he? How do we destroy him? What do I have to do?" Gerry blurted out, hardly able to contain himself.

"One thing at a time, son. Hold your horses. Listen to me for a moment. I'll explain everything," Moot interrupted, placing his hand on Gerry's shoulder. Gerry was beginning to feel he could now trust this old man, despite what he had made him go through.

Chapter Eight

"Several hundred years ago, the owner of Carswell Hall, a Mr Ronald Carswell was murdered. He was murdered by the inhabitants of the village surrounding the old Hall. For years he had tormented the townsfolk, treating them badly, overcharging them rent, and often throwing them out of their homes for the flimsiest of reasons. Families were often ruined by his wicked actions. The local people hated him. They pleaded to him for better treatment, but he scorned them. His was a world of wealth and privilege. The people had no one to turn to. The Law was no help, as Carswell himself was the Law. He controlled the local police and all the local magistrates. Finally they decided to take matters into their own hands. A group of men broke into the hall late one night, captured Carswell, tied him up and threw him into the lake, drowning him. Just before he disappeared under the water, it was reported that he had sworn to exact revenge on the town. He swore he wouldn't rest until it was destroyed. Ever since, he has not been at rest. From time to time he returns from wherever he goes, to cause harm to this town and the people who live here. He will never rest until he destroys the town . . . or until somebody stops him."

Gerry sat in silence listening to the old man's tale, absorbing every word.

Moot continued, "I was on to him all those years ago. I had discovered how to control him, how to kill him, to put him to rest forever. I thought I had done it, destroyed his spirit. I returned home, to this very house, excited by what I believed I had achieved. But as I sat here in my chair, all those years ago, I sensed that he was still around. It was the last thing I felt. He killed me."

"But what happened, how did you fail?" Gerry asked impatiently.

"I don't know," the old man replied. "I simply don't know. The secret of dealing with him and spirits like him is the light. They cannot exist in the light. They are spirits of the dark. They draw their strength from the dark. They are evil. If you can catch them in the light and keep them there, their power weakens and fades until their power disappears and their spirit dies, never to return again. I had set it all up. I had him there, in front of me. His spirit seemed to wither and expire in front of my very eyes. But somehow he must have survived."

"So what do we do now?" Gerry asked

"We try again. This time we'll make sure it's done correctly. The last time I couldn't have held him in the light for long enough. I won't make the same mistake twice," Moot replied, clenching his two fists and thumping the arms of his chair.

"But what do you want me to do?" Gerry asked, still a little puzzled by his role in the whole affair.

"First I have a some work for you. If you look in the cellar of this house, you will find a number of large mirrors, and a half a dozen or so spotlights. You will also find a small diesel generator. I have checked, it's still working. I need you to take them all up to the old hall tomorrow as soon as you have finished school. It'll take you a few trips so start as soon as you get home. We have to be ready before it gets dark," Moot instructed the boy.

"I understand what the spotlights are for, but why the mirrors?" Gerry asked.

The old man continued, "These spirits cannot stand their own image. We have to hang the mirrors on the doors and windows of the sitting room of Carswell Hall. That's where we will trap him. With the mirrors there, he will be unable to escape through the doors or windows. With the lights and the mirrors, the light will be so strong, and his image so visible every way he turns, he will be powerless. If we can keep him there for 60 seconds, the light will destroy his spirit and he will be gone forever."

"But he's a ghost, won't he just pass through the walls? Surely he doesn't need doors or windows?" Gerry asked, bemused.

Moot started to laugh. "This is the real world Gerry, not some movie. He is a spirit, but his body is real, you can touch it, feel it. He has many powers, but he cannot walk through walls. This is no Casper we are dealing with," Moot replied, shaking his head.

Gerry looked at the old man. His old face was becoming animated, purposeful.

"And what about you Mr Moot? What happens to you?" the young boy asked, looking up to the old man in the rocking chair, beginning to feel sorry for him.

"He is the reason that I am trapped here. Trapped in this chair, in this house, in this street, in this town. I cannot rest, until he does. Get rid of him and you get rid of me too. Two for the price of one, eh Gerry? Not bad, eh?" Moot replied reaching over and gripping Gerry's shoulder.

Gerry gave a nervous smile and nodded his head. He felt the old man's sadness.

"Now listen up, while I go over our plan in more detail. When you get to the hall tomorrow, I want you to ..."

For the next hour Moot went through his instructions to Gerry over and over again. When he was finished Gerry returned home with his mind racing. Moot had impressed on him how dangerous his mission was. He climbed into bed feeling sure he would be awake all night, going over the plan for tomorrow, time and time again in his mind. However, he hadn't realised how exhausted he was, and he was asleep within seconds. Again, he didn't notice the shadow of the rocking chair on the wall above his bed. This time it seemed to be looking after him, protecting him.

Chapter Nine

The next day, he managed to avoid getting into trouble with Mrs Martin. He paid just enough attention in class to get by, but it was very difficult. How could he concentrate on anything with the night he had ahead of him? He had almost told Stevie a couple of times but had managed to stop himself. As soon as school was over he sped straight home, got changed, grabbed his bike and headed over to the old derelict house to start his work.

Carswell Hall sat behind some trees, at the far end of the park at the bottom of Gerry's street. Gerry had looked up at it many times when he and his pals were down the park playing football. He had never ventured anywhere near it. It was one of those places nobody wanted to go near. Although it had lain empty for years, the local council had kept it reasonably well maintained in a hope of selling it to some wealthy businessman, or to some property developer who could turn it into a leisure centre, health farm, hotel or something similar. They never had managed to sell it. For some reason, no sale had ever gone through. As soon as a prospective buyer came close to buying, he would strangely pull out.

It took Gerry seven trips, back and forth to the hall, pulling a loaded cart behind his bike, to get all the gear from Moot's cellar to the house. It had taken him a lot longer than planned as he had needed to keep looking out to make sure his parents weren't around. He had told them he was going to see a movie with Stevie.

Chapter Nine

As he unloaded the last load in front of the large main door of the hall, he looked at his watch: 6.30 pm. He was late. It would take him at least an hour to set everything up. It would be dark by 8 pm. Moot had told him he must have everything in place before it got dark. He had been quite serious about that. It was going to be tight. He pulled the large door open. It took all his strength to pull it back far enough for him to squeeze in. From the other side he pushed it open further to give him enough room to get the equipment in. The creaking of the door echoed through the empty house.

Gerry looked around. He suddenly felt very alone. In front of him the large entrance hall led to the base of a wide, sweeping staircase. At the top of the staircase, looking straight back down to the main door, hung a large portrait of a fierce looking man astride a marvellous white horse. The image seemed to dominate the whole room. Gerry wondered if the portrait was of Ronald Carswell, the murdered master of the house.

To the left of the hall was the sitting room. That was where Gerry had to set up the equipment. He walked towards the large panelled door. He entered slowly. The room was dark. There was one large window at the head of the room and there were two doors leading to the entrance hall and one leading to the adjoining library. Four possible routes of escape for the evil spirit. Gerry had to set the mirrors up at these points. One mirror was nailed to the back of each of the doors and two were perched up against the window. The lights had to be positioned all around the room, targeted at the very centre. Gerry worked away without stopping. The last thing he did was to attach the cable from the lights to the generator. This proved more difficult than it looked as the generator socket was full of dirt and the plug kept falling off. After Gerry cleaned it out, the plug held in place. Everything was ready, just as Moot had instructed him. One turn of the generator key and the place would be filled with light.

Gerry reached into his pocket. Moot had told him to leave the key in position ready for the right moment. There was nothing there. Gerry tried his other pocket. No key!

Gerry's heart was beating so loudly he was sure it would burst.

"Where on earth . . . ?" he hissed, becoming angry with himself. How could he be so careless and stupid? Gerry ran out into the entrance hall and out of the large door. He ran over to his cart, looking for the key. It was nowhere to be seen. He had to find it. Suddenly something moved in the bush to his left. Gerry froze. He leaned down behind his old cart. Slowly a small black cat emerged from behind the bush, looked over at Gerry and walked away.

Gerry let out a long sigh and stood up. He could barely see the cat as it wandered away, and Gerry suddenly realised how dark it had become. He entered the door again. But as he walked through, he immediately saw the figure standing at the top of the stairs. Whoever it was hadn't noticed Gerry. He was standing facing the large portrait. Gerry slipped quietly behind a cabinet to the side of the door.

Gerry peered round the side of the cabinet. He studied the man at the top of the stairs. It was the same man in the portrait – same long black boots, riding trousers, red jacket and plumed hat. He couldn't see his face but he was sure this was him. This was Ronald Carswell.

Gerry looked over to the sitting room. There was no way he would make it over without Carswell spotting him. He knew he was in real trouble now. He tried to think, but as he leaned back his head hit a sword hung on the wall behind him. The clattering noise filled the room. Carswell spun round. Gerry cowered behind the cabinet.

"Who is there?" Carswell demanded, his eyes scanning the hall below him. "Come out and die, whoever dares enter my house," the evil master bellowed.

Gerry couldn't stop from shaking. He was surely done for.

He could hear Carswell starting to walk down the stairs, his heavy riding boots sending a chilling echo around the house.

Suddenly, the main door burst open.

Gerry looked over. He could only see the legs of somebody standing in the entrance.

"Ahah . . . Moot. You again? Go away, get out of my house you scum," Carswell sneered. Gerry was too afraid to look.

"Carswell, your time has come. This time I will not fail." Moot retorted. His voice full of authority.

"Don't make me laugh, old man. Be gone and leave me alone, I am tired of you. Get out of my sight!" Carswell demanded.

Gerry poked his head out. Moot was now walking straight towards Carswell. Carswell had reached the bottom of the stairs.

The two enemies stared at each other. Then without any warning, Carswell swung his arm up, smashing it into the old man's face, knocking him back to the ground.

Carswell started to laugh. A loud chilling laugh that filled the whole house. Carswell lifted the old man up and flung him hard against the wall.

"I cannot kill you again, but I can make your body ache till it cries out for mercy."

Carswell shouted, standing over Moot ready to strike again.

Gerry couldn't watch any more. He had to do something. He ran out from behind the cabinet and sprinted to the sitting room door.

Carswell spun round just as Gerry leapt through the door.

"What is this? Another intruder. You will die too," Carswell bellowed. He looked down at Moot and snarled, "I will deal with you later."

Gerry was cowering behind the large sofa, as Carswell entered the sitting room. The room was almost in pitch black darkness. Gerry started to crawl slowly away from the door, trying to remain hidden. As his fingers felt the way, he suddenly touched something cold. He looked down. The generator key! It must have dropped out of his pocket when he was preparing the room. He grabbed it tightly.

Carswell surveyed the room, trying to find the intruder. He started to make out the strange pieces of equipment spread out in front of him.

"You're wasting your time, idiots. Show yourself, you coward," the ancient fiend yelled threateningly, beginning to realise what the intruders where up to.

Gerry tensed himself, the key in his hand. He had to get to the generator. Carswell stood in the doorway, the generator was unnoticed in the darkness to his side.

Suddenly Carswell went flying, sprawling to the ground. Moot staggered through the door, an iron poker in his hand. He threw himself on top of Carswell.

"Quick, Gerry, the lights!" Moot shouted.

Gerry seized his chance. In a flash he was at the generator. He inserted the key and turned it. The engine rumbled into life. In an instant the room was filled with light. Gerry covered his eyes, the brightness blinding him.

Carswell screamed out, an agonising deathly scream. He lifted Moot and threw him across the room. Gerry could just make out the writhing figure staggering around in the middle of the room. Everywhere Carswell turned there were lights. Their beams penetrated his body, his very soul. The deranged spirit leapt to the large window, planning to throw himself through it, but staggered back as he confronted his own evil image.

Gerry looked at the sitting room door. It was still open. Carswell noticed at the same time. Carswell sprang from the other side of the room, making for his last possible exit. He seemed to fly through the air. Gerry slammed it shut just in time. Carswell screamed, as his own distorted face stared back at him from the mirror behind the door.

Gerry watched as the fiendish image in front of him wailed and staggered about. Finally he fell to the ground, his face twisted in agony. Gradually his image began to fade, melting away, till eventually it was gone, and there was no more trace of him. The noises of Carswell's screams and cries died away and the room fell silent. Gerry waited, holding his breath. He had to be sure. The bright lights continued to burn.

"It's done, son. He's gone. You did it," Moot gasped, climbing to his feet.

"After three hundred years, the village is rid of him."

Gerry couldn't move. His body was frozen, pinned to the sitting room wall.

The old man put his arms around the young ghostbuster,

"Come on, son, Let's go home."

Chapter Ten

Gerry leaned back in his chair, and thought back to that night all those years ago. He had never forgotten the adventure of almost 50 years ago now, when he had battled the evil spirit at Carswell Hall. It still made him feel good, so proud. It was such a long time ago, he thought

He looked at the newspaper cutting on his office wall.

"Cup victory for local school. 5-4 in penalty shoot-out."

Gerry smiled to himself. The memories flooded back.

The door burst open. A young fresh-faced kid ran in, disturbing Gerry's thoughts

"Mr Editor . . . Mr Editor . . . .there's been a break-in at the computer factory. We have just heard it on the police radio."

"Jimmy, you cover it. It's about time you had a go," Gerry replied, waving the lad away.

"Thanks Mr Editor, I won't let you down," the young aspiring reporter replied excitedly.

"Jimmy, don't call me Mr Editor, how many times do I have to tell you? It's Gerry," Gerry snapped back.

"Yes, sir, Mr Editor," Jimmy replied, rushing back out the door.

Gerry watched the young reporter leave. He smiled. He could remember his first assignment. It was to report on a measles epidemic at his old school. He had ended up catching the disease himself. He was in bed for a week. The old editor hadn't been impressed.

Mrs Cullen, Gerry's secretary, poked her head in the door.

"We need more staff, Gerry. We're not coping. It's chaos out here. Oh and that's Mr Collins from the antique shop just off the phone. He's going to deliver the rocking chair to your house in twenty minutes."

"Thanks, Linda. I am leaving right now, and I promise I'll sort out the staff soon," Gerry replied, packing up his briefcase, trying to appease his secretary.

The weekend before, Gerry had spotted an old rocking chair that looked exactly like the one Mr Moot had owned all those years ago. He couldn't resist buying it. Ever since, he couldn't stop thinking about his ghostbusting adventure with Moot up at the old hall. It was strange, as he hadn't thought about those days for ages. In fact the last time it had entered his mind was over twenty years previously when he had bought and renovated old Moot's house opposite his own parents' house. Now he seemed obsessed by it all over again. He couldn't get it out of his mind.

"Right, that's me off, Linda. See you tomorrow." Gerry waved as he made his way through the office.

"Bye, Gerry," Mrs Cullen replied without raising her head.

Gerry arrived home just in time to see Mr Collins lift the chair from the back of his van.

"Over there Stan. On the porch," Gerry pointed to the spot where the chair was to sit.

"This thing weighs a ton, Gerry. Real good old wood. Solid as your head," Mr Collins groaned as he lifted the chair on to the porch.

"It's built to last forever, Stan, just like me," Gerry replied, knocking his head mockingly.

"This'll last a lot longer than you, believe me, mate," Mr Collins added wiping his brow after his efforts.

"Thanks a lot, Stan. There's plenty of life left in these old bones yet. I'd still give you a run for your money round the block, eh . . . fancy a try?" Gerry challenged his good friend.

"Are you kidding? Lifting that chair has just about done me in. I'm off home to put my feet up." Mr Collins replied, shaking his head and climbing into his van.

"Bye, Stan. Thanks a lot," Gerry shouted, waving him off.

Gerry stepped up onto the porch and was just about to try out his new purchase, when the phone started to ring.

"Blast . . . !" he muttered as he made his way inside.

"Hello, Gerry Tooms," he snapped down the phone.

"Mr Tooms, Sammy here, sorry to disturb you at home sir, but I didn't know what to do."

Sammy was Gerry's sub-editor and was doing the evening shift back at the office.

"What's up, Sammy, couldn't it wait?" Gerry asked, irritated at having to do newspaper work at home.

"Mr Tooms, we have received reports of disturbances up at the old Carswell Hall. The labourers who were working up there are talking about all sorts of strange happenings. One of them is missing. I want to send someone up but we don't have anybody. What should I do, sir?

Gerry started to laugh.

"Sammy, the number of times we have

been up at that old house over the years with all sorts of weird and wonderful tails . . . . it will be a wild goose chase as usual. Any ghosts up there are long gone," he said, smiling to himself and thinking of his previous exploits.

"But . . . Sir . . ." Sammy started

"Leave it for now, Sammy. We'll send up somebody in the morning. It can wait till then," Gerry interrupted.

"OK, boss," Sammy agreed reluctantly.

Gerry put the phone down. His smile disappeared. Carswell Hall still gave him the creeps. Over the last few days a number of strange reports had come in from more and more people describing strange sights and sounds. One or two reports a year about the hall were commonplace ever since he joined the newspaper. They had all turned out to be crank calls. Suddenly however reports were coming in thick and fast. Maybe it was time to investigate further.

Gerry thought about his staff. There simply weren't enough of them to go around. He decided it was time to get more help. He smiled. "We need a new "ghostbuster", well a "ghost-story buster" at least," he thought.

His thoughts were interrupted by a noise from the porch. Gerry walked out and looked around. There was nobody there. Gerry looked over to his newly purchased rocking chair. It was swaying back and forth.

"Funny," Gerry thought, "there's not a breath of wind in the air."

"Ah well, time to get the feet up and rest my weary bones," he muttered to himself as he sat down on the old chair. He started to rock the chair slowly, its movement relaxing him, clearing his mind. His eyelids began to fall slowly over his tired eyes. He started to feel dizzy, his stomach began to churn. He felt a nagging pain in his neck, and then it was gone. His eyes began to close.

Before he drifted off, he looked up. He caught sight of a young boy watching him from a window across the road. A frightened familiar-looking boy, staring from behind his curtains.

Chapter Eleven

Gerry awoke with a start. He didn't feel good at all. He looked at his watch. It had stopped. He must have slept on the chair all night. He quickly changed and got ready for work. As he wandered around the house, something seemed different. He felt quite different. There was a strange musty smell. Gerry looked around. The house looked quite dirty, unkempt, the decoration somehow seemed old and out of date. Gerry shook his head.

"This place needs some attention," he thought, walking out the door and locking it behind him.

As he went down his path, he noticed

the weeds that had sprung up, the grass that had grown so tall.

"I have been spending too much time at work," he thought.

Twenty minutes later, Gerry was at his desk. The main office was busy, but nobody had disturbed him. It made a pleasant change. Usually his office was full of people as soon as he walked through the door. He welcomed the peace and quiet this morning. He wasn't feeling himself, he hadn't felt good since he woke up. He closed his eyes trying to stop his head spinning.

"What are we doing here?"

Gerry opened his eyes. Opposite him stood a young lad, looking somewhat uncertain. He tried to gather his thoughts. He was looking for more staff. Mrs Cullen must have arranged an interview. He sat up and pointed to a chair in the corner.

Chapter Eleven

"This is my office, son, make yourself at home. Grab a chair," Gerry spoke the words automatically. They seemed strangely familiar. He looked at the young boy in front of him. He was sure he recognised the boy, but he couldn't place him. His head was still spinning. Something wasn't right. What was wrong with him? It was as if he was floating in some dream.

Gerry looked beyond the boy, out of his office window, into the main office. It was full of activity. He could see Linda standing at her desk talking to one of the reporters. He started to shout to her, "Linda, come in a minute." His throat was dry he needed a drink.

"Linda, come here please," he repeated loudly. She didn't move, continuing to speak with the reporter. She seemed agitated, upset.

Gerry sat back in his chair and closed

his eyes. Something was wrong with him. He looked at the boy.

"Go home, son. Something has come up. I'll be in touch when I need you," Gerry said without opening his eyes. He heard the noise of the door opening and closing. He was alone.

Gerry stood up and walked to his office door.

"Linda, a minute please," he said, calling over to his secretary. Still she continued talking.

"Linda, for goodness sake," Gerry raised his voice impatiently, walking over to her desk.

Mrs Cullen still didn't react. Gerry leaned over to touch her arm. His hand passed straight through. He tried again. The same thing. It was as if he was in a dream. He couldn't believe it. She didn't seem to know he was there. He looked around the office. Nobody seemed to know he was there. It was as if he was invisible.

Gerry shouted at the top of his voice: "Will somebody listen to me?"

Everyone carried on without any reaction. Gerry noticed two or three of the women crying, consoling each other. He ran over to them.

"What's wrong? What's happened?" He asked. It was useless. They couldn't hear him.

Gerry was confused. It was as if he was in another world, some twilight world. He closed his eyes, and shook himself, trying to break out of the nightmare he seemed to be in. It was no good. He fell back into a nearby chair and buried his head in his hands. As he stared at the desk in front of him, the words on the newspaper lying there hit him like a bolt.

"Editor dies in freak accident. Falls from rocking chair – broken neck."

Gerry couldn't believe his eyes. Below the headline was his own picture.

"No . . . NO!" he cried, beating his hands against the desk.

Gerry stood up. He couldn't believe this was happening. He was sure it was some joke, some bad dream. He ran through the office and out into the entrance hall. He burst through the toilet door, found a sink and turned the tap on. He felt sick. He started to pour the cold refreshing water over his face. It felt good. He looked at himself in the mirror. He looked terrible. His face was grey and his eyes swollen.

He caught sight of his office ID badge, hanging from his shirt pocket. His name in the reflection looked strange. He studied it. He could read "TOOM S" clearly in the reflection. That shouldn't have been possible.

The blood drained from his face. He removed the badge and held it in his hand. "TOOMS" had become "Z MOOT"

"But . . . but this is impossible," Gerry thought to himself.

"No, it isn't. It is quite possible," a voice from behind whispered, chillingly in his ear.

Gerry spun around. The figure in front of him was unmistakable.

"Carswell . . . you? It can't . . ." Gerry tried to speak, the words sticking in his throat.

"Yes, it's me. It's our time again," Carswell replied, his face twisted in an evil scowl.

Gerry's head began to spin. He had to escape. He had to get out of there. His vision went out of focus. He felt himself falling.

When he opened his eyes again it was dark. He was sitting in his rocking chair on the old derelict porch. A yellow light from the street lamp cast a strange glow across the street. He looked up at the window opposite. He could see him standing there. He knew exactly how the boy would feel, what he was thinking. He remembered it well. The boy was looking down again. Gerry would need his help. He would have to contact him. He smiled at the boy. He raised his hand slowly and began to wave.

The time had come again. They had come full circle.

We hope you enjoyed this story from the Creepers series. Here are some other titles for you to collect:

The Hooded Hangman
Stage Fright
The Rocking CHair
The Entertainer
The Golden Goblet
The Gravedigger

This series was conceived by Edgar J. Hyde and much of the text was provided by his minions under slavish conditions and pain of death! Thankfully none of the minions defied their master and so we can say "thank you" to them for toughing it out and making this series possible

Titles available in Creepers

Series One
The Piano
The Scarecrow
Beggar Boy
Mirror Mirror
Ghost Writer
The Wishing Well

Series Two
Dr Death
The Ghostly Soldier
Blood On Tap
Edgar Escapes
Happy Halloween
Soul Harvest

Titles available in Creepers

Series Three
Payback Time
Rag And Bone Man
Cold Kisser
Pen Pals
The Sold Souls
Noisy Neighbours

Series Four
The Gravedigger
The Rocking Chair
Stage Fright
The Golden Goblet
The Entertainer
The Hooded Hangman